W9-AVB-196

2924

HURRAY FOR
ALI BABA BERNSTEIN

BY JOHANNA HURWITZ

The Adventures of Ali Baba Bernstein
Aldo Applesauce
Aldo Ice Cream
Baseball Fever
Busybody Nora
Class Clown
The Cold and Hot Winter
DeDe Takes Charge!
The Hot and Cold Summer
Hurricane Elaine
The Law of Gravity
Much Ado About Aldo
New Neighbors for Nora
Nora and Mrs. Mind-Your-Own-Business
Once I Was a Plum Tree
The Rabbi's Girls
Rip-Roaring Russell
Russell Rides Again
Russell Sprouts
Superduper Teddy
Teacher's Pet
Tough-Luck Karen
Yellow Blue Jay

CHINA CASTLE 2ND FL.
EGG ROLL KING
KING BURGERS
BROS., CO.
ROYAL JEWELRY
CROWN INC
GOWNS INC.
UNDERWEAR KING
PRINCE LEATHERS

HURRAY FOR

ALI BABA BERNSTEIN

BY

JOHANNA HURWITZ

ILLUSTRATED BY GAIL OWENS

Morrow Junior Books
New York

Hurray for my friends
Helen and David Stephenson

Chapter 6, "Ali Baba and the Mystery of the Missing Circus Tickets," originally appeared in a different version as "Rosie Relkin's Raincoat" in *In Another World and Other Stories*, edited by Mark W. Aulls, Ed.D., and Michael F. Graves, Ph.D.
Inquiries should be addressed to
William Morrow and Company, Inc.,
105 Madison Avenue,
New York, NY 10016.

Printed in the United States of America.
1 2 3 4 5 6 7 8 9 10

Library of Congress Cataloging-in-Publication Data
Hurwitz, Johanna.
Hurray for Ali Baba Bernstein /by Johanna Hurwitz ; illustrated
by Gail Owens.
p. cm.
Summary: The further adventures and misadventures of nine-year-old
Ali Baba Bernstein.
ISBN 0-688-08241-6. ISBN 0-688-08242-4 (lib. bdg.)
[1. City and town life—Fiction. 2. Humorous stories.]
I. Owens, Gail, ill. II. Title.
PZ7.H9574Hr 1989
[Fic]—dc19 88-19107 CIP AC

CONTENTS

1. ALI BABA BREAKS THE RULES

Last year when David Bernstein was in third grade, there had been three other boys named David in his class. There were David Katz, David Rodriguez, and David Shapiro. David Bernstein did not like that a bit. It was much too confusing. Then, one day when he was reading a book called *The Arabian Nights,* he discovered a wonderful name: Ali Baba. There were no other Ali Babas in his class. And as far as

David Bernstein knew, there were no other Ali Babas in his school. It was the perfect new name for a boy who wanted to be different.

David Bernstein had told his parents, his teacher, and his classmates to call him Ali Baba. His teacher had been surprised by this name changing in the midst of the school year. However, there was no rule about it, and so with time, she did.

Now Ali Baba Bernstein was nine years, four months, and seven days old. His mother said he was old enough to act his age and accept the name he had been given when he was born. That was easy for her to say. She didn't sit in a fourth-grade classroom from Monday to Friday and hear other people being called her name over and over again. Even though David Katz had moved during the summer, there were still four Davids in the class. Now there was a new boy named David Lee, who had transferred from another school.

Ali Baba Bernstein was determined that if he ever changed schools, he would have his parents investigate the names of his new classmates first. And in the meantime he would continue to use the name Ali Baba. It made him feel important and it made him feel special. He liked that.

On the Friday morning in September that Ali Baba Bernstein was nine years, four months, and eleven days old, his fourth-grade class was scheduled to take a trip to the public library.

Ms. Melrose had told the students about the library visit several times during the week. Each time she concluded her comments with the words, "Be sure to bring your library card to school with you on Friday." She wanted each of them to borrow a biography for their first report. A biography, she explained, was the story of someone's life. Ali Baba hoped that someday someone would write a book about the story of his life.

Ali Baba always carried his library card in the same plastic case that held his monthly bus pass and an emergency card with the telephone number of his father's office. So when he got on the bus to go to school that Friday morning, it never occurred to him that he had a problem. But as the bus neared the school he put his hand into his back pocket and removed the little plastic case. He admired his green bus pass and wondered what color he would get next month. Perhaps October would be red.

Then Ali Baba flipped open the different compartments of the case and looked for his library card. It was not there. How could he have lost it?

"Hey, come on," Natalie called to Ali Baba as she was getting off the bus. "This is our stop."

Natalie was a second-grader who lived on the same street as Ali Baba. On the bus to school each day she always sat or stood as close to Ali Baba as she could. Usually she just stared at him. Ali Baba knew that she had a crush on him, because a couple of the girls in Natalie's class had told him. He generally pretended to ignore her, but he often watched her out of the corner of his eye. She was the first girl who liked him.

Ali Baba stuffed the plastic case back into his pocket and readjusted his backpack as he got off the bus. Where could his library card be?

"I love Fridays," said Natalie as the two of them walked in the direction of the school.

Ali Baba didn't answer. He was too busy trying to figure out the location of his missing library card. He was sure he hadn't lost it. He remembered going to the library and checking out a book quite recently. And suddenly Ali Baba realized what had happened. The librarian had stuck his card in the pocket of the book he had borrowed that day. The card was still in the pocket, and the book was on the floor under his bed at home.

"Don't you like Fridays?" asked Natalie. When Ali Baba didn't respond, she asked, "Don't you like to talk to me? It's not my fault that I'm not as old as you are."

"I don't care how old you are," said Ali Baba. "I've got a problem." He looked at the small girl walking beside him. "Do you have a library card?" he asked her.

"Sure," said Natalie, nodding her head. "I got it when I was in first grade."

"Would you let me borrow it?"

Natalie looked less certain. "The librarian said that we should never, ever let anyone else use our card, because then we'd have to pay if the book got lost." She looked at Ali Baba. "But if you cross your heart and hope to die that you'll return all the books on time, I'd let *you* use my card."

"Super," said Ali Baba, smiling at Natalie with relief. Who would have guessed that it would be so useful to have a second-grade girl with a crush on him? "My class is going to the library this morning, and Ms. Melrose will have a fit if she finds out I left my card at home."

"Oh," said Natalie as they reached the entrance of the school. "My card is at home, too. I thought you wanted to use it this afternoon when school was over."

"That's no help," grumbled Ali Baba.

"Good-bye," Natalie said, waving to Ali Baba as they parted.

Ali Baba was too preoccupied about his library card to respond.

Practically the first thing that Ms. Melrose said to the class was, "Does everyone here have a library card?"

Ali Baba knew he should raise his hand and tell her that he did not have his card. But the way the teacher worded the question kept him from responding. Yes. He had his library card. At home. If she had said, "Do all of you have your library card here with you right this minute?" then he would have had to admit that he didn't.

"Good," said Ms. Melrose, beaming at her students. "Then everyone can borrow a book at the public library." Ms. Melrose was the prettiest teacher Ali Baba had ever had. She looked as if she should be on TV and not teaching at P.S. 35. In a way, Ali Baba thought that he felt the same way about Ms. Melrose that Natalie felt about him. He liked to sit in class and watch her. And whenever the teacher smiled, he felt like smiling, too. So how could he possibly tell her something now that would bring a frown to her face?

Ali Baba looked around the classroom. He wondered who would share their card with him. If only Roger Zucker was in his class this year, he would have agreed in a second because he was Ali Baba's best friend. Tony Mancuso sat with Ali Baba at lunch every day.

He might have let him use his card, except Tony had been absent from school the day before. Looking around him now, Ali Baba saw that Tony was still absent.

There was no time to talk with anyone because Ms. Melrose was rushing through the morning's routine. The students stood and recited the Pledge of Allegiance and took their Friday morning spelling quiz. Then Annabel Singer's mother was at the classroom door. She was the class mother who was going to accompany the fourth-graders when they went to the library.

Ali Baba got an idea. While all the other students were putting their notebooks away, he went up to Ms. Melrose and asked permission to go to the office. "I have to phone my mother," he said.

"Is there a problem?" she asked him.

"It's something personal," he said.

"All right. Hurry right back."

Ali Baba rushed down the hall to the front office. He told Mrs. Greene, the secretary, that he had to make a call home. Luckily no one else was waiting to use the telephone.

Sometimes there was a whole line of students who had forgotten their lunches or their consent slips or money for special things. Ali Baba was going to ask his mother to meet him at the library and to bring his card. It was a good plan, except that no one answered the telephone. He counted twelve rings, although he knew his mother always answered it by the third ring. Even when she was sitting right next to the telephone, she always waited until the third ring to pick it up.

He thought of calling his grandparents, but he knew that even if they were home, it was too much to expect them to travel up to his apartment and find his library card and then bring it to the library. His father wouldn't want to do that, either.

So Ali Baba went back to the classroom where the students were all lined up and waiting for him.

"You're sure everything is all right?" asked the teacher.

Ali Baba was almost going to tell her that he had left his card at home. But he was afraid she would ask him why he hadn't told her earlier, and he didn't know what he would answer. So he just nodded his head as he put his jacket on and got on the end of the line. He didn't have a partner, but he was too busy thinking about his library card to care.

The public library was ten blocks away from the school. Ali Baba's home was ten blocks away from the library. The library was exactly in the middle between his home and the school. It was because he lived twenty blocks from school, which was a full mile, that he got the student bus pass from the city every month.

As the students walked toward the library, Ali Baba had another idea. He would slip away from the class and go home. Then he could get his card and meet the class at the library. A whole classful of students walking down the street moved much more slowly than he could on his own. If he hurried, he could meet the class at the library, and no one would even know that he had been gone.

Luckily Ali Baba was at the end of the line of students. And luckily, too, he didn't have a partner. So it was quite easy to duck behind into a doorway as the students turned a corner. He waited till they were halfway up the next street before he dashed out of his hiding place. Then Ali Baba set off at a run. It was a lovely autumn day, and he felt good as he ran along the streets to his home. At some corners he had to wait for the traffic light to turn green before he could cross, but at other corners he did not have to break his stride at all. It was fun running. If he didn't have a heavy backpack, he could run to and from school every day, he thought.

By the time he reached his house, Ali Baba was winded. He stood panting for breath as he waited for the elevator. "My goodness, why aren't you in school?" asked one of the older women who lived in the building. Ali Baba wasn't sure what he would have answered, but he was still trying to catch his breath and so no words came out, and the woman walked away without an answer.

Ali Baba had his own key. It was taped to a piece of cardboard and kept inside the plastic folder with his bus pass. It was there for an emergency, and finally Ali Baba had an emer-

gency. He rarely had an opportunity to use his key, so he was pleased to have this chance to let himself into the apartment.

"Mom?" he called out, just in case his mother had returned home. But there was no answer. He ran to his bedroom and looked under his bed. Sure enough, there was his library book right where he had left it. And sure enough, inside the pocket of the book was his card.

Ali Baba glanced at the clock in his room as he rushed out. It was only ten-twenty. His class had left the school building just before ten o'clock. They were scheduled to be at the library at ten-thirty. If he ran to the library as quickly as he had run to his house, he would make it without a problem. He had to waste a whole minute waiting for the elevator. When it arrived, fat Mr. Salmon, who lived on the floor above, was in it. The two looked at each other but didn't exchange any words.

Once out of the building, Ali Baba set off at a run. He thought he would ask his father how one went about entering the New York City Marathon. With this experience behind him, he felt he could do it easily.

Ali Baba had hoped that he would arrive at the library at the same time as his class. But when he reached the entrance of the public library, there was no sign of his classmates. He was either too early or too late. He looked at his watch and saw that it was twenty-five minutes to eleven. He was late. By now Ms. Melrose and the fourth-graders were upstairs in the children's room. He wondered if anyone had noticed that he was missing. He could tiptoe inside and sit in the back. Or else he could wait in the hallway to the children's room, and when everyone got up to look at the books, he could join them then. He decided that was what he would do.

Ali Baba climbed up the steps to the library door and tried to open it. It was locked. A sign on the door said that the library was closed until noon. That meant that when his class arrived, someone had opened the door especially for them. If he rang the doorbell to the library, it would call attention to his lateness. Worse, Ms. Melrose would know that he had left the class when they were walking to the library.

Ali Baba sat down on the top step and tried to think what to do. He could wait until his class left the library and join them then. He was sure that by that time Ms. Melrose would realize that he was missing. And, of course, he wouldn't have a book to discuss in class that afternoon. It was a big problem.

A big brown United Parcel truck pulled up in front of the library. Ali Baba watched as the driver got out of his seat and rummaged around in the back of the truck. That was a great job, he thought, driving all around the city and bringing packages to people. The driver stepped out of the truck and set a large carton on the ground. He put a second, smaller carton down on top of the first.

"Do you need help?" Ali Baba called to him.

"I have two packages to deliver here," said the man.

Ali Baba ran down the steps and picked up the smaller box. "Let me do it," he offered.

The man picked up the big carton and followed Ali Baba up the library steps and pushed the bell.

"What are you doing here?" asked the driver as they waited for someone to answer the door. "Shouldn't you be in school?"

"My class is visiting the library," Ali Baba explained.

Just then the door opened. The driver and Ali Baba walked inside with the packages. "You have to sign here," the man told the librarian as he handed him a clipboard.

Ali Baba put the smaller package on the front desk. Then he walked quickly and quietly toward the steps leading up to the children's room. He could hear the children's librarian talking as he neared the top. She was telling a story to the class. The lights were turned off and the room was in semidarkness. The librarian was telling a spooky Halloween story. All eyes were on the librarian. It was dark, but not too dark for Ali Baba to see his way to an empty chair in the back row. He tried to sit down quietly, but the scraping of the chair legs against the tile floor made a noise that seemed extra loud because of the silence. Ali Baba stared straight ahead at the librarian.

"You did it!" shrieked the librarian, and she pointed her finger at Ali Baba.

Ali Baba jumped with fright. "No I didn't," he said, gasping. "I mean, I didn't mean to, but I couldn't help it. I forgot my card."

Everyone was laughing. The librarian's shout had been the last line of the story. She wasn't accusing Ali Baba of anything, but nevertheless he had given himself away.

The lights were turned on and the children were told to look for books. The librarian led the way to the biography section and began to help everyone select books. Ms. Melrose went over to Ali Baba. Even with a frown on her face she looked pretty, he thought.

"Where were you?" she asked.

"I went to get my library card," he explained.

"You know you are not to leave school without permission," said Ms. Melrose.

"But I did have permission. The whole class left together. I just went home and got my card before I came here," said Ali Baba. It didn't seem like such a big crime to him.

"During the school day you are under my jurisdiction," said the teacher. "You can't just rush home when you please. I didn't know where you were. I was very concerned about you."

"I thought you wouldn't notice. I wasn't gone very long," said Ali Baba.

"Of course I noticed," said Ms. Melrose. "I wouldn't be a very good teacher if I didn't notice that a student of mine had disappeared. I had to phone the school office and report you missing."

"Did you think I was kidnapped?" asked Ali Baba. "Are the police looking for me?" It was an exciting possibility.

"I didn't know," admitted the teacher. "I had better call the school and tell them that you've turned up. Now go and pick out a book. I will have to think about how you are going to be punished."

"Punished?" asked Ali Baba. "All I did was go home and get my library card."

"Why didn't you tell me that you had left your card at home this morning when I asked the class?" asked the teacher.

"I didn't want you to be angry," said Ali Baba.

"So I am angry now instead," she said, but

she smiled as she said it. "I think your punishment is that you will have to be my partner all the way back to the school building. I don't want to have to worry about losing you again."

"All the way back to school?" asked Ali Baba.

"All the way," said Ms. Melrose.

Ali Baba joined his classmates at the bookshelves. Ms. Melrose helped him to select two biographies. One was about George Washington and the other was about Abraham Lincoln. "Neither of these men told lies," she said. "They were both known for their honesty."

"Maybe neither of them left their library cards inside the pockets of library books underneath their beds," said Ali Baba. "Maybe they would have told a lie then."

Ms. Melrose went over to the shelves and selected a third book. "Perhaps you should read this biography instead," she said, handing it to Ali Baba. "It's about a man with a vivid imagination. The world needs people like that."

Ali Baba looked at the book. It was about Thomas Edison.

"Did he ever tell lies?" he asked.

"I don't know," admitted Ms. Melrose. "You will have to read the book to find out."

The students lined up and checked out their books. Then they put on their jackets and walked down the steps out of the library building. This time, instead of being at the end of the line, Ali Baba was up at the front. He walked all the way back to school next to Ms. Melrose. It was supposed to be a punishment, but it wasn't bad at all. Ali Baba thought he wouldn't mind being punished like that every day.

2. ALI BABA AND THE CASE OF KELLY'S DELI

Ever since he was very young, Ali Baba had been intrigued by mysteries. He loved television programs and movies that showed how mysteries were solved. He tried to imitate the detectives and the private eyes that he had seen on the screen. He knew that a good detective kept his eyes open at all times. No detail was too insignificant. Everything was a potential clue. And so every day at school and at home, Ali Baba watched carefully and noted all. He considered himself the private eye of the public school. Who knew? Perhaps someday he would solve a really big mystery and make a real name for himself.

Ali Baba was always on the lookout for things that seemed suspicious. Recently he had become aware that his neighbor Mr. Salmon had been behaving strangely. Ali Baba lived on the sixth floor, and several times in recent weeks, when he had ridden in the elevator, Mr. Salmon had been there, too. Mr. Salmon was a large, balding man with a mustache and a small beard. His wife was a tiny woman only half his size.

Once Mr. and Mrs. Bernstein had been speaking about the Salmons and Ali Baba learned that Mr. Salmon worked at home as a C.P.A. That in itself was quite strange. Ali Baba didn't know what C.P.A. meant, but he didn't think it could be good. If his neighbor was a doctor or a lawyer or a salesman, wouldn't he come out and admit it? Hiding his business behind some mysterious initials seemed very suspicious to Ali Baba.

The first few times he had found himself in the elevator with Mr. Salmon, Ali Baba occupied himself with trying to figure out what the letters C.P.A. stood for. Captain of the Police Association? Criminal and Pirate Activities? Chief of Private Arsonists? It was about the third or the fourth time that they were riding up together in the elevator that Ali Baba realized that Mr. Salmon always got off on the fifth floor. There was nothing wrong with getting off on the fifth floor of the building if you lived there. But Mr. Salmon lived on the seventh floor. Certainly this was most peculiar and suspicious behavior.

Ali Baba decided that the next time he was in the elevator with Mr. Salmon, he would get off on the fourth floor and quietly walk up the stairs and spy on his neighbor. He also kept a lookout for Mr. Salmon when he was out on the street. That's when he discovered that Mr. Salmon spent a lot of his time in Kelly's Deli.

Kelly's Deli was just around the corner from where Ali Baba lived. His mother, who did most of her shopping once a week in the large supermarket three blocks away, nevertheless always seemed to be out of groceries at crucial moments. Hardly a day went by that she didn't need an extra quart of milk or a half-dozen eggs. It was a nuisance to have to run these errands all the time, but it did give Ali Baba a chance to keep his eye on the neighborhood. Everyone used Kelly's Deli. So Ali Baba wasn't surprised the first time he discovered Mr. Salmon in the delicatessen when he went on one of his mother's emergency errands.

As Ali Baba paid for the jar of mayonnaise his mother had sent him to get, he watched Mr. Salmon. He had bought a wedge of cheesecake from the row of cakes that were displayed behind the glass divider at the counter. Ali Baba had often admired the cakes. There was a fudgy chocolate one that looked especially delicious, but his mother had never, ever bought any of them. Now he watched as Mr. Salmon removed the cheesecake from the paper bag in which it had been placed and began to devour it right inside the store. It was gone in about three mouthfuls.

Ali Baba watched as Mr. Salmon licked his

SPECIALS
POTATO SALAD
MACARONI SALAD 95¢
SLICED BALOGNA
TURKEY
ROAST

upper lip, then took a handkerchief from his pocket and rubbed his mustache and lips. Ali Baba felt thirsty at the thought of eating a whole piece of cake without a single drop of milk to wash it down. However, Mr. Salmon did not seem to miss a glass of milk, and after crushing the paper bag, he set it on the counter and walked out of the store.

Cheesecake Partners Association?

The second time he met Mr. Salmon in Kelly's Deli, the man was eating again. When Ali Baba walked into the store, he saw Mr. Salmon standing off to the side and holding a large slice of carrot cake on a paper plate. What made the carrot cake look so delicious was that it had fluffy white frosting on top and between its layers. Mr. Salmon succeeded in eating the carrot cake in just a few bites. It was almost suppertime, and Ali Baba thought he would die of hunger as he watched Mr. Salmon chew up his last mouthful of cake.

When Ali Baba got back to his building, Mr. Salmon was waiting for the elevator. The man and the boy got into it together. Ali Baba pushed six, which was his floor. Then he noticed that Mr. Salmon had pushed five. It reminded him that he was going to spy on his neighbor, and so he pushed number four. The elevator started up, and when it reached the fourth floor, the door opened. If Mr. Salmon thought it strange that Ali Baba got off at the wrong floor, he didn't comment.

Ali Baba dashed up the stairs and was poised near the top step, panting for breath, when the elevator stopped on the fifth floor. The door opened, and although he could not see him, he heard Mr. Salmon get out. The elevator doors closed again, and Ali Baba listened. He wondered what Mr. Salmon was going to do on the fifth floor. Did he stop to visit someone? Was he going to pass on some secret messages or a secret parcel?

He heard Mr. Salmon's footsteps. The older man had begun walking up the next flight of stairs. Was it possible that he knew that Ali Baba was hiding nearby, so he wasn't going to deliver his message after all? Slowly Mr. Salmon climbed up step after step. And quietly, waiting until his neighbor was a flight ahead of him and therefore not in view, Ali

Baba followed. Mr. Salmon paused briefly on the sixth floor and then continued to the seventh. Ali Baba followed behind. On the seventh floor he crouched behind the stairwell and listened as Mr. Salmon opened a door with a key. Even without checking, Ali Baba knew the man was opening his own door. Why had he gotten off at the fifth floor? Had he realized that he was being followed? There was something fishy about Mr. Salmon and his activities.

On the day that Ali Baba Bernstein was nine years, four months, and twenty-nine days old, his mother again asked him to go to Kelly's Deli. She wanted a jar of olives to use in a new recipe she was going to make for supper. As Ali Baba didn't like olives, he knew he would spend half his mealtime picking the olives out of his portion. It seemed unfair that he had to go and purchase the olives if he wouldn't be eating them. Still, once he arrived at Kelly's Deli, he was glad he was there.

Standing in front of the glass case, studying the various pastries, was Mr. Salmon.

"The cheesecake is extra fresh today. We

just got it in this morning," said the man behind the counter, who Ali Baba had always assumed was Mr. Kelly.

Mr. Salmon shook his head. "I don't feel in the mood for cheesecake just now," he said.

"How about a nice slice of pecan pie?" offered Mr. Kelly.

Mr. Salmon again shook his head. "No, not today."

Suddenly an idea occurred to Ali Baba. Could it be that the cakes and pies in Kelly's Deli were a sort of code? Did carrot cake mean one thing and cheesecake mean another? If Mr. Salmon selected a particular dessert, would he really be telling Mr. Kelly about some sort of a deal? Perhaps cheesecake meant "Meet me at the bank" or "I have the documents for you."

Ali Baba watched as Mr. Salmon chose a slice of the fudgy chocolate cake. It had three layers, and each was attached to the others by a thick frosting that made Ali Baba's mouth water just looking at it.

C.P.A.—Chocolate, pure and appetizing? Crime Patrol Anonymous? Citizens for a

Proud America? Convicted Prisoners Association? The possibilities were endless. And the number of cakes on display seemed endless, too. How could Ali Baba ever break the code and discover just what Mr. Salmon was up to?

He was so busy trying to work out the mystery of the cake code that he bought olives without pimientos, although his mother had especially reminded him that she wanted olives with pimientos. As a result, when Ali Baba got home, he was told to go back to Kelly's Deli again. As he went down in the elevator, he wondered where Mr. Salmon was. Although he had left Kelly's Deli, he hadn't returned home after devouring his chocolate cake. If he had, Ali Baba would have seen him. When Ali Baba entered Kelly's Deli for the second time that day, his question was answered. Mr. Salmon hadn't gone home. Although Mr. Salmon had left the delicatessen before Ali Baba, he had, like Ali Baba, returned there again.

C.P.A.—Counterfeit Presidential Agency? Ali Baba just couldn't figure out what was going on. Mr. Salmon wasn't buying any cake this time.

"I want a pound of the health salad," he said, pointing to a display of cut-up fresh vegetables.

That seemed a very strange order coming from Mr. Salmon. He must have realized that Ali Baba was listening to him and changed his tactics. Or else the change from desserts to salad meant a complete change in Mr. Salmon's plans. Ali Baba was becoming more and more certain he was watching a spy in action.

"Anything else?" asked Mr. Kelly.

"Yes. I'll have a quarter of a pound of sliced turkey breast."

It was stranger and stranger.

Mr. Salmon paid for his purchases and left the store. Ali Baba quickly explained to Mr. Kelly about his error. Luckily olives with pimientos cost the same as olives without. So it was a simple matter to exchange the one for the other, and Ali Baba was out of the shop within seconds. He raced home, hoping to catch up with Mr. Salmon.

The heavy, bearded Mr. Salmon was waiting at the elevator. He was holding the paper bag with his purchases. The elevator stopped at the ground floor. Mrs. Cummings, who lived on the third floor, got off. She nodded to Mr. Salmon. Ali Baba wondered if she knew what he was up to. "Nice day," said Mr. Salmon with a smile. That was suspicious, too. It looked as if it might rain any second.

Mr. Salmon got into the elevator and pushed five. Ali Baba resisted the desire to push four. His mother was waiting for the olives, and besides, Mr. Salmon was already suspicious of him. So Ali Baba pushed six. When the elevator reached the fifth floor, Mr. Salmon sighed. He did not get out. Instead, he leaned over and pushed seven, which was his correct floor. Now Ali Baba was more suspicious than ever. What was this man up to?

C.P.A.—Chocolate Pastry Association? Communist Party of America! Ali Baba stood looking at his bearded neighbor. The elevator reached the sixth floor and Ali Baba got out quickly. He knew he had to do something, but he didn't know what. He was convinced that while he had been buying olives, important American secrets had been delivered to Kelly of Kelly's Deli. Health salad instead of cake. It had to mean something!

Mrs. Bernstein was waiting impatiently for the olives. "I have to slice them up and mix them in the casserole," she explained as she took the bag from her son.

She tried to open the narrow jar. Her face turned quite red with effort, but she did not succeed. Ali Baba watched as she tapped the sides of the lid with a knife. Then she tried to turn the lid. Again she failed. Next she ran hot water over the jar. But it didn't seem to make any difference. The lid refused to come off. Ali Baba grinned. Maybe he wouldn't have to pick olives out of his supper after all.

"You try," said his mother. "Maybe you'll have better luck."

It wasn't fair to ask him to prove his superior strength by opening a jar of olives that he wished would stay shut. But in the end it didn't matter. Although he put all his might into it, Ali Baba also failed to open the jar of olives.

Mrs. Bernstein sighed. "Your father won't be home until six o'clock," she said. "I need this jar opened now."

"Do you want me to take it back to Kelly's Deli?" asked Ali Baba. It would be embarrassing to have to ask Mr. Kelly to open the jar for him. But perhaps Mr. Salmon would be in the store passing some new message.

"I have a better idea," said Mrs. Bernstein. "Mr. Salmon works at home. He should be upstairs now. Take this jar up and ask him if he can open it for us."

"Mr. Salmon?"

"Yes. You know, he lives right above us, in apartment 7G."

Of course, Ali Baba knew that. He just couldn't imagine asking an enemy agent to open a jar of olives. Still, it would be a chance to peek into his apartment. Ali Baba took the jar from his mother and walked up the flight of stairs to apartment 7G. He rang the doorbell and waited.

"Who is it?" called Mr. Salmon from inside. He opened the little peephole in the door to look out. Perhaps he was expecting another spy.

Ali Baba waved the jar of olives so that Mr. Salmon could see it. "My mother asked if you could open this," he said.

The door opened. Mr. Salmon looked

much fatter when he wasn't wearing a jacket. He looked too fat to be a spy, but maybe that was part of his disguise. Who would expect a fat, slow-moving man like him to be a C.P.A.?

Surprisingly, Mr. Salmon was strong enough to open the jar. He removed the lid, then removed one of the olives, too. He popped it into his mouth. "Just a small payment," he said as he chewed it up. And then he took another.

"I don't like olives," said Ali Baba.

"Unfortunately, I like everything," Mr. Salmon said with a sigh. "That is my downfall."

Ali Baba stood in the doorway and wondered what Mr. Salmon meant. Did his downfall mean that he was going off to jail? Had someone else detected him passing secret messages at Kelly's Deli?

"I joined OA, but it hasn't helped at all," Mr. Salmon explained. He took another olive, then handed the jar to Ali Baba.

"What is OA?" asked Ali Baba. Since Mr. Salmon seemed ready to spill the beans, Ali

7G
MIAMI

Baba was not going to stand around guessing what those letters meant.

"Overeaters Anonymous. I've been put on a strict diet, and I'm supposed to do exercise every day, too. You've probably noticed that I sometimes get off the elevator on the fifth floor. The doctor said that if I walked up those two floors every time I come into the building, I'd burn up five hundred calories in a week. Five hundred calories! I can consume five hundred calories in three minutes. It's a losing battle."

Mr. Salmon looked so unhappy that Ali Baba handed him the olive jar again. Perhaps another olive would cheer him up.

Mr. Salmon shook his head. "Do you know how many calories are in one stuffed olive?" he asked.

"No."

"Seventeen," said Mr. Salmon.

"That's not much," said Ali Baba.

"True. But no one ever eats just one olive. They're like peanuts or potato chips. Eat one and you want another."

Ali Baba knew that wasn't true. He loved

peanuts and potato chips, and he could eat dozens of them. But he couldn't eat one olive.

"I'm a C.P.A. I work with numbers all day. But half the time when I'm supposed to be working on someone's accounts, I'm really counting up the number of calories I consumed. I have charts, graphs, everything. And they all show just one thing—I eat too much."

"I don't think you're too fat," Ali Baba lied. He was suddenly feeling sorry for this huge man who was always hungry.

"Tell that to my wife. The first thing she is going to ask me when she gets home from work is if I bought any cake at Kelly's Deli."

"Hey," said Ali Baba suddenly. "Would you be interested in running with me? I did some running the other day and it was fun. I thought I'd go running in Riverside Park. But my father said he didn't want me to go off running by myself. If we went together, I wouldn't be alone, and you would lose a lot of weight."

"You know, that's not a bad idea," said Mr. Salmon. "I even bought a pair of running shoes once. But mostly I wear them when I go out to the deli."

"You'll never lose weight that way," warned Ali Baba.

"I know." Mr. Salmon sighed.

"I guess I better take these to my mother," said Ali Baba. He had suddenly realized that he was still holding the olive jar in his hand.

Mr. Salmon nodded. "Sorry if I chewed off your ear," he said.

Ali Baba rubbed his ears. "It's okay," he said. "You helped me solve a mystery." He now knew that chocolate cake and cheesecake were not part of a secret code after all. They just meant that Mr. Salmon loved to eat.

"Really? What sort of mystery was that?"

"Never mind," said Ali Baba. "But could you just tell me what C.P.A. means?"

"Sure," said Mr. Salmon. "I'm an accountant. C.P.A. means Certified Public Accountant."

"Oh. Thanks. And thanks for opening the jar, too. I'll ring your bell when I get home from school tomorrow. We can go running then, if you want."

"Perfect," said Mr. Salmon.

Ali Baba Bernstein walked back down the stairs with the half-empty jar of olives. It was a relief to know that his neighbor wasn't an enemy agent after all. Still, he was a little sorry, too. It had been exciting to consider the possibility. But at least he had found himself a running partner. And who knew? Perhaps when he was out running, he would find another mystery to solve.

3. ALI BABA BERNSTEIN, KING FOR A DAY

On the Tuesday in November that Ali Baba Bernstein was nine years, five months, and twenty-seven days old, school was closed. It was Election Day, and while citizens aged eighteen and over were voting, and the teachers at his school were holding an all-day conference, the students were free to do as they wished. At least that's what Ali Baba thought. His mother had a different idea.

"We're going shopping today," she informed her son when he was eating his breakfast. "You need new underwear, and I need new towels."

"I wanted to play with Roger today," Ali Baba protested. "I don't want to go shopping."

"You played with Roger yesterday, and you'll see him in school tomorrow," said Mrs. Bernstein.

"But today's a school holiday. Who wants to buy underwear on a holiday?" Ali Baba grumbled. It didn't seem fair that his mother should make plans for him. Sometimes he wished he were king of the world. Then no one could tell him what to do.

"It won't be so bad," his mother tried to assure him. "We'll have lunch out, and we're going to a part of New York where you've never been. Maybe you'll see a few new things."

"New things? What new things?" asked Ali Baba crossly. "New underwear?"

"One never knows. Just keep your eyes open," suggested Mrs. Bernstein.

Ali Baba always kept his eyes open, except when he was sleeping. But his mother was right. Even though there was nothing he hated more than shopping, going to a new neighborhood might prove revealing. There was always the possibility of observing some mysterious goings-on that he would have missed had he stayed home. And so, with that thought, Ali Baba finished his bowl of cornflakes and finished his complaining.

They took a subway to lower Manhattan. "I heard of a store that has wonderful bargains," Mrs. Bernstein told her son over the rumble of the subway train.

Ali Baba nodded his head as he looked around. The train was filled with people going off to unknown destinations. He wondered if anyone else in the subway car was in need of new underwear. He wondered if anyone was off on a secret mission. Most of the people looked half-asleep, but perhaps that was the way you had to look if you were on a mission. If you looked alert and eager, you might give yourself away.

They got off the train at Houston Street and

walked two blocks. Ali Baba smiled to himself as they passed several Chinese restaurants. Maybe they could go to one of them for lunch. He thought of himself crunching down on a mouthful of crisp Chinese noodles, and he licked his lips in anticipation.

Mrs. Bernstein stopped and pulled out a piece of paper from her pocket. On it she had written the address of the store she was looking for. "It must be at the end of this street," she said, and sure enough, in another moment they had reached their first destination: Barney's Bargains—The Home of the Underwear King.

Who would have imagined a king on this street, thought Ali Baba as his mother opened the door and motioned for him to follow. Inside, behind the counter, was a balding man with a big smile. Ali Baba supposed he was Barney the Underwear King, even though he was only wearing a plaid flannel sport shirt and a pair of slacks. He'd always assumed that kings wore long flowing robes and crowns on their heads.

"My son needs new underwear," Mrs.

Bernstein said. "Undershirts and pants. He needs socks, too."

The king smiled at Ali Baba. "Young man, take off your jacket. Let me see what size you need."

"Yes, Your Majesty," Ali Baba replied as he unzipped his jacket and took it off.

Mrs. Bernstein gave her son a poke. "Behave yourself," she hissed at him.

But the Underwear King beamed. "I like you," he said to Ali Baba. "You have a sense of humor. That's a good thing to have, believe me."

Ali Baba nodded as the Underwear King took a tape measure and held it up against his shoulders, then measured his waist.

"Here you are," he said, showing Mrs. Bernstein packages of undershirts and pants. "Now, as to socks, do you want hundred-percent cotton, or do you want nylon? There's a special on cotton tube socks," he added quickly. "Three pairs for the price of two, today only."

"We'll take six pairs of the ones on sale," said Ali Baba's mother.

"Smart woman!" said King Barney. "Anything else? How about pajamas? T-shirts? What about a fancy dress shirt for a special occasion?"

Mrs. Bernstein shook her head. "No, he doesn't need anything else today."

"What about you? Panty hose? Slips? Bras? I have everything here at fantastic prices."

"No, not today," said Mrs. Bernstein. "Perhaps I'll be back another time for those things."

"Your husband? He must need something. Shirts, socks, a nice bathrobe, a new tie?"

"Nothing. No, this is all," said Ali Baba's mother. "What do I owe you for these things?"

The Underwear King began adding up the prices of the underwear and the socks. He showed Mrs. Bernstein the total, and she paid him.

"Come back again soon," he said as they took the shopping bag he gave them.

"Yes, Your Highness," said Ali Baba, bowing low. It wasn't every day that he met a king, even if it was only a king of underwear.

BOYS 2-8
BOYS 10-16
SHIRT SALE
SUPER BARGAIN BIN

"Now the towels," said Mrs. Bernstein when they were back out on the street.

"Is there a towel king?" asked Ali Baba.

"Don't be silly," said his mother. "I was very embarrassed the way you spoke to the man in that shop. He isn't a real king. I was afraid you were going to get down on your knees and kiss his hand, the way you were acting."

Ali Baba hit himself on the forehead. "I forgot," he said. "I saw it in a movie once, but I forgot to do it."

"This is the United States. We don't have royalty here," said his mother. "That man is no more a king than you or I."

Ali Baba didn't say anything, but he didn't agree with his mother. How could someone call himself a king if he wasn't? Of course, they had seen the Underwear King.

They hadn't walked more than half a block when Ali Baba spotted another Chinese restaurant. The sign in the window read EGG ROLL KING.

"Look at that!" said Ali Baba. "If the owner of that restaurant came from China, he could have been a king there."

"In China they had emperors, not kings, and they don't have them anymore," said Mrs. Bernstein.

Ali Baba was not convinced. He liked the idea that in this section of New York there was royalty.

Ali Baba found the towel store incredibly dull. Who could enjoy an entire store filled only with towels and sheets and pillowcases? There were some blankets, too, but none of those things were exciting. Ali Baba leaned against one of the counters and waited while his mother deliberated between sea-blue towels and sky-blue ones.

Finally she made a decision in favor of sea blue, only to discover that there were no matching washcloths left in that shade. What a waste of time, Ali Baba thought. When the sky-blue towels and washcloths were packaged and paid for, they walked out of the shop.

"When are we going to eat?" asked Ali Baba.

"Soon," said Mrs. Bernstein. "I just want to look in that pocketbook store we passed on the way here."

"You didn't say anything about buying a pocketbook," complained Ali Baba.

"I didn't know there was a sale there," said his mother.

As they walked back, Ali Baba discovered a store that he hadn't noticed before. The Donut King was just across the street from the pocketbook store.

"Can I go and buy a doughnut?" begged Ali Baba. "I'm going to die from hunger."

"All right," agreed his mother. "Here is some money. But don't leave the store. Wait right there and I'll meet you."

Ali Baba took the money his mother handed him. When the light turned green, he crossed the street, eager to eat a doughnut and to meet another king.

Inside the doughnut shop was a counter with three people at it, drinking cups of coffee and eating doughnuts. Behind the counter there was no king. Standing there, pouring coffee, was an elderly woman. Perhaps she was the king's mother. Or his wife.

Ali Baba sat down on one of the empty stools and studied the list of doughnuts: sugared or honey-glazed, chocolate-covered or plain, filled with jelly or cream or custard, round or cruller-shaped. The possibilities seemed endless.

"What do you want?" asked the woman.

"First I want to meet the king," said Ali Baba. "Then I'll have a doughnut."

"What king?"

"The Donut King. I already met the Underwear King this morning, and now I want to meet the Donut King."

"You mean Harry? He's the owner. He has the flu, and he won't be coming in today. What about the doughnut? What kind do you want?" asked the woman.

It was a disappointment not to meet the king, but Ali Baba found solace in a chocolate-covered doughnut.

"Do you want some milk?" asked the woman. The pin on her stained white jacket read MILDRED.

"Hmm," said Ali Baba, nodding his head in agreement.

Mildred poured him a glass of milk.

"Tell me about Harry," said Ali Baba. "Is he like a king at all?"

"Well, he has a gold tooth," Mildred said,

laughing. "It's right in front," she said, pointing to one of her own front teeth to demonstrate. "So you can't miss it when you are talking to him. But otherwise he's a pretty ordinary guy. Just like everyone else around here."

"I wish I could see a real king," said Ali Baba. "You know, the kind they have in storybooks."

"That kind don't exist anymore, except in Europe or someplace," said Mildred.

Ali Baba sighed. It was too bad. Perhaps his mother was right after all.

The door to the shop opened, letting in a gust of cold air and Mrs. Bernstein.

"Look at this," she said as she held out a tan leather pocketbook. "It was a real bargain."

"Do you want a doughnut?" asked Mildred, looking at Mrs. Bernstein and the new pocketbook.

"No thanks. I just came to pick up my son."

"He's a real sweet kid," said Mildred. "You're doing a good job bringing him up."

"Why, thanks," said Mrs. Bernstein.

Ali Baba licked the chocolate off his fingers and got down from the stool. "Okay, Mom. I'm done," he said.

He paid Mildred for his doughnut and milk, and even remembered to leave her a quarter for a tip. Then they were on their way again.

"Now will we go and have lunch?" asked Ali Baba.

"Lunch? You just had a snack," said his mother.

"But I'm still hungry."

"We'll have lunch in a little while," said Mrs. Bernstein. "But as long as we're down in this neighborhood, I want to see if I can pick up a nice sweater for your father."

Ali Baba was getting bored as they walked on to the sweater store. However, his mood lifted quickly when he saw where they were headed: The Sweater Palace. Who lived in a palace? A king! Ali Baba couldn't wait to enter the store.

There were two men working behind the shop's huge counters. Behind them were shelves and shelves of sweaters in every shade imaginable. Mrs. Bernstein began speaking with one of the men. Ali Baba could see that this was going to take a long time. However, being in a palace, he was determined to locate the king. He walked over to the unoccupied salesman and addressed him.

"Are you the king of the Sweater Palace?" he asked.

"My brother and I are co-owners," said the man, smiling. "Does that make me a king?"

"Which of you is the oldest? The oldest son always inherits the kingdom and the throne," said Ali Baba, remembering the fairy tales he had read when he was younger.

"It just so happens we are twins," said the salesman. "I'm Fred, and that's my brother Ed over there. Our parents were so excited when we were born that they couldn't even remember which of us was born first."

"No kidding?" said Ali Baba. He turned to look at the other twin, who was speaking to Mrs. Bernstein. He was showing her the various types of sweaters that he had in stock. The two men did look alike. They matched like two sleeves on the same sweater.

"I've noticed a lot of kings in this neighborhood," said Ali Baba. "There was an Underwear King named Barney, an Egg Roll King, and a Donut King who has the flu."

Fred nodded his head. "Any man can be a king," he agreed. "It's no big deal. Around here you could call yourself a king, too, if you wanted to."

"I'd like that," said Ali Baba. "I could be King of the Davids. In the Bible there was a King David. But I would be King of all the Davids."

"Fine, if that's what you want," said Fred.

"Wouldn't it be great to be a real king over everyone?" asked Ali Baba. "To be in charge of the whole world?"

Fred shrugged his shoulders. "Some kings were good, and some were bad. But the worst thing about kings was that they had their job for life. You couldn't vote them out of office like we can vote for the president or the governor or the mayor. And another thing—their sons automatically became the next king, even if they were stupid or wicked."

"I hadn't thought of that," Ali Baba said.

"Listen, kid, I can't talk anymore. I just

remembered something," said Fred. He called over to his brother. "Ed, I'm going off to vote. I'll be back in ten or fifteen minutes."

Ed looked up from the pile of sweaters he had set out on the counter. He nodded to his brother. Ali Baba marveled that they did look very, very much alike. He walked over to his mother. The sweaters looked very much alike to him, too. He wondered how she would ever be able to make a decision. But eventually, just as Ali Baba thought he would collapse with exhaustion, she made her choice. Ed rang up the sale and put the sweater in a box.

"So long, Ed," said Ali Baba as they walked toward the door.

"How did you know my name?" Ed asked.

"I know a lot of things," said Ali Baba.

"Now we'll stop for lunch," said Mrs. Bernstein when they were out in the cold November air again. "Look," she said, pointing to a store just ahead of them. "We can eat there if you want." The sign read BURGER KING.

Ali Baba shook his head. "No," he said. "Couldn't we have Chinese food? Please."

So the two of them crossed the street, and on the next block they found the China Castle. It was the perfect place for lunch, even though it wasn't a real castle, and Ali Baba wasn't a real king.

4. ALI BABA MEETS SANTA CLAUS

In the first place, Ali Baba Bernstein was nine years, six months, and twenty-three days old, much too old to believe in the existence of Santa Claus. In the second place, Ali Baba was Jewish. That meant that he and his parents did not celebrate Christmas. Still, he knew all about Santa Claus from storybooks and television shows and from the tales his classmates told. Nevertheless, it was still a major surprise to get off the bus on his way home from school and to see Santa Claus walking toward him.

Ali Baba was not alone. Natalie Gomez, the second-grader who lived on his street, got off the bus at the same stop and stood beside him.

"Look over there!" said Ali Baba, pointing toward the short, heavyset man with a thick head of white hair and a long, flowing white beard. "He sure looks like Santa Claus, doesn't he?"

Natalie's jaw dropped open. For a moment she didn't say a word to Ali Baba. Even though he was wearing dark slacks and a tweed overcoat, she also recognized the man. "It *is* Santa Claus," she whispered. "I know it's him. I would recognize him anywhere." Her voice was full of awe. After all, it wasn't every day that you met Santa Claus walking down Broadway. "He lives at the North Pole," Natalie reminded Ali Baba. "That's a lot of bus and subway stops away from here."

"It's halfway around the world," Ali Baba informed her.

"I wonder why he isn't wearing his red

suit?" Natalie asked as the man came toward them.

"Use your head," Ali Baba told the little girl. "If he wore his bright red suit with the white fur trim, everyone would be chasing after him. That's a disguise that he has on now."

"Let's follow him," said Ali Baba as the man approached still closer.

"We can't do that," Natalie said with a gasp.

"Why not?" asked Ali Baba. "Don't you want to see where he's going?"

Natalie nodded her head. "But he might get angry. Then he won't bring us anything for Christmas."

"Well, I don't have to worry about that," said Ali Baba. "And I want to see where he goes. Maybe he's inspecting the toy shops around here or something."

He turned to follow the bearded man, but he did not have to go far at all.

"Look," said Natalie as Santa Claus entered a barbershop. "He's going for a haircut."

Ali Baba and Natalie stood outside the shop and peeked through the window. They

watched as the famous man got into one of the chairs. The barber put a towel around his neck and began snipping at his hair.

"Wait till I tell the kids in my class about this," Natalie exclaimed. "They won't believe it!"

They watched as the barber trimmed Santa Claus's beard.

"Do you think the barber knows who he is?" asked Natalie.

"Nope," said Ali Baba with certainty. "Grown-ups don't even believe in Santa Claus."

"You believe in him, don't you?" said Natalie. "Just because you're two years older than me doesn't mean *you* can't believe in him."

"It's different with me," Ali Baba reminded Natalie. "Don't forget that I don't celebrate Christmas."

"You mean, you don't get any presents at all?" asked Natalie, shocked.

"Sure I get presents. I get birthday presents and Hanukkah presents and presents from my grandparents just because they love me, even if there isn't a holiday. Sometimes my father brings something home for me because he saw it in a store and he thought I would like it and he didn't want to wait until it was my birthday. Last week my mother bought me a new book that she saw on sale in a bookstore because she knew I'd read other books by the same writer. I get loads of presents."

"But no Christmas presents from Santa Claus, right?" asked Natalie. "Why don't you ask him about it when he comes out?" she suggested.

"You mean, you think I should ask Santa Claus why Jewish kids don't get Christmas presents like you do?"

Natalie nodded her head. "I don't think it's fair that you don't get anything. You should ask him about it."

"That's a good idea. I will," said Ali Baba. "I bet the other Jewish kids at school will want to know about it, too."

He spoke with confidence. But as he watched the barber remove the towel from around Santa Claus's neck and shake out all the little white hairs, he began to feel a bit nervous. If he made Santa Claus angry, then he certainly would never get any gifts from him in the future. Of course, he would be no worse off than he was now.

Ali Baba and Natalie watched as Santa Claus put on his heavy coat and paid the barber. They stepped aside as the door opened and Santa Claus came back out into the street.

It was unusual for Ali Baba to be at a loss for words. Luckily, as he stood trying to think of how to address him, Natalie spoke up.

"Hi!" she said, grinning up at Santa Claus.

"Hi," the man responded.

"We know who you are," she said proudly. "We guessed it."

"You did?" said Santa Claus, pretending to be surprised. "How were you able to do that?"

"It's the way you look," said Ali Baba, feeling more confident now that the ice was broken and conversation had begun. "No disguise can hide who you really are."

"Well, you won't tell anyone, will you?" asked the man.

"Can't I tell my friends at school that I saw you?" begged Natalie.

"It doesn't matter," Ali Baba told her. "No

one will believe you anyhow. Don't you think I'm right?" he asked Santa Claus.

"Listen, kids," said the man. "I hate to say this, but haven't you been taught by your parents or by your teachers that you should never speak to strangers?"

"Of course," said Ali Baba. "But we wouldn't exactly call you a stranger. Just about every kid in the world knows who you are."

"Really? And who is that?" asked the man.

"Do you want us to say your name out loud?" asked Ali Baba. "Someone might overhear us."

"That's true," the man agreed. He smiled at Ali Baba and Natalie. "Listen," he said, "I was just about to have a cup of coffee. Do you want to join me?"

"Do we have to have coffee?" asked Natalie. "I'm too little to drink coffee."

"Me too," Ali Baba admitted reluctantly. "But we could get hot chocolate or something else."

"Good thinking," said the man as they entered the luncheonette. He noticed the backpacks that both Ali Baba and Natalie were wearing. "Were you on your way home from school just now?" he asked them.

"Yep. We noticed you the minute we got off the bus," said Ali Baba. "I recognized you first," he said, bragging.

"Here," said the man, reaching into his pocket and handing them each a quarter. "Go phone your parents and tell them where you are. I don't want them to be worrying about you."

Ali Baba saw the wisdom in this suggestion. He went to the phone booth with Natalie and called his mother.

"I'm going to be a little bit late today," he said importantly. "I stopped to have hot chocolate with Natalie Gomez."

He didn't mention the presence of Santa Claus. He knew his mother would not believe him anyhow. Then Ali Baba dialed the phone number that Natalie recited for him. She was too short to reach the phone. He handed her the telephone receiver. Like Ali Baba before her, she reported that she was having hot chocolate at the luncheonette, but she did not mention Santa Claus.

"Okay. I'll come right home when I'm done," she promised her mother.

Then they went back to the counter where Santa Claus was waiting for them. A cup of coffee and two hot chocolates were waiting on the red Formica countertop.

The man removed a pen from his pocket. He handed it to Ali Baba and slid a paper napkin over to him, too. "Here," he said, "write down who you think I am."

Ali Baba nodded. "Smart," he said admiringly. "That way nobody can hear us." It was a trick he had seen on television. It wasn't easy to write on the napkin without tearing the soft paper, but Ali Baba managed to write out "Santa Claus."

The man began to laugh. The sound wasn't exactly the jolly "ho ho ho" that Ali Baba and Natalie had heard on TV and in the movies, but they realized that he had to disguise his true manner when he was out in public this way.

"So you guessed that was who I am?" the man said.

"Sure. It was easy. You're a dead giveaway.

SANDWICHES

If you want my advice, you should shave your beard when you're going traveling. I'm surprised that hundreds of people haven't already stopped you," said Ali Baba.

"If I shaved off my beard, it wouldn't grow back in time for Christmas," argued Santa Claus.

"You could wear a fake one, like all the fake Santa Clauses do. No one would know the difference," Ali Baba suggested.

"He has an important question to ask you," Natalie said, looking up from her hot chocolate. There was a mustache of dark brown chocolate across the top of her lip.

"What is it?" Santa Claus asked Ali Baba.

Ali Baba blushed a deep red. He wanted to ask his question, but he didn't want to seem rude.

"Go on," said Natalie, giving Ali Baba a nudge. "This may be your only chance."

"Well, it's like this," said Ali Baba. "You see, I'm Jewish. And I wondered if you ever thought about bringing presents to Jewish kids on Christmas."

"It doesn't seem fair otherwise," said Natalie.

"Have you asked your parents about this?" asked Santa Claus.

"Sure. They explained that Christmas is a Christian holiday. And I can understand that part. But still, I thought that I should ask you now that I've met you in person. Don't you ever have any leftover things?"

"Tell me," said Santa Claus, "do you ever get any other kinds of presents instead of Christmas ones?"

"Oh sure," said Ali Baba. And then he listed for Santa Claus, just as he had earlier for Natalie, all the types of gifts that he received over the year.

"Well, young man, it certainly doesn't sound as if you're deprived. So I think you'll understand when I say that after all the Christmas presents are distributed each year, it always seems important to give those left over to children who wouldn't get anything from anyone else."

"You mean, like orphans?" asked Ali Baba.

"That's right. Orphans or children in hospitals. Children who need presents because they don't have the things you already have.

I don't mean things like games and toys, but things like loving parents and good health and a promising future ahead of you. Those are the most important things in the world," Santa Claus explained. "And they aren't the kind of things that I'm able to give away." He paused for a moment. "I wish I could," he said.

"But you bring presents to Natalie," said Ali Baba. "She has loving parents and good health." He didn't want to seem greedy, but he did want to clarify the situation once and for all.

"It's like this," said Santa Claus, looking a little uncomfortable. "My assignment is to distribute presents to the children who celebrate Christmas. I was assured that you would get other gifts from other sources. And from what you tell me, that's exactly how it is. So, in the end, you both have a happy holiday season." He swallowed the last of his coffee. "You understand, don't you?"

Ali Baba nodded his head. "Do you have any message for other kids that you want us to pass along?" he asked.

"We're not supposed to say we met him," Natalie reminded Ali Baba.

"Right," the man agreed. "But you can just set a good example." He thought for a moment. "By being friends, by being nice to others, by caring."

"Sam Cooperman!" a voice called out. "What a surprise to see you here!"

A woman entering the luncheonette came over to them and began talking to Santa Claus. "I was going to phone you," she said. "Paul and I wanted to invite you over for dinner." She looked at Ali Baba and Natalie. "My goodness, are these your grandchildren?" she asked.

"These are some young friends of mine," Santa Claus explained.

"We have to go now," said Ali Baba, getting off his stool. He pulled at Natalie, who was busy tearing her paper napkin into strips. Ali Baba watched as Santa Claus held out his hand and took Natalie's small hand in his. "In case I don't get a chance to see you again," he said, "Merry Christmas."

"Merry Christmas," said Natalie. She stood

still for a second, then impulsively put her arms around Santa Claus and gave him a kiss.

Ali Baba didn't plan to kiss Santa Claus. But he held out his hand to shake with him, man to man. "It was very nice meeting you," he said politely.

"It was my pleasure," said Santa Claus.

"And thank you very much for the hot chocolate," Ali Baba remembered to add at the last minute.

Santa Claus gestured to Ali Baba to come closer. He leaned over and whispered something in his ear. Ali Baba nodded his head and grinned.

The woman sat down on the stool that Natalie had vacated. "So tell me, what are you doing now?"

Ali Baba stood for a minute listening.

"When I finish my coffee, I'm going to the barbershop," Santa Claus told his friend.

Ali Baba was just about to protest that he had just come from the barbershop when Santa Claus made another statement. "I've decided that it's time to shave off my beard," he said.

"For goodness sake. After all these years, why are you going to do that?" asked the woman.

"Too many people seem to recognize me these days," he said. And at that moment both Ali Baba and Natalie Gomez noticed the famous twinkle in Santa Claus's eyes.

"Did you hear that woman call him Sam Cooperman?" said Natalie all of a sudden as they walked along the street. "Maybe he wasn't Santa Claus after all."

"Don't be silly," said Ali Baba. "He has to have an alias, doesn't he? And he even kept the right initials, S. C. Believe me, we just had hot chocolate with Santa Claus."

"Too bad we can't tell anyone about it." Natalie sighed, convinced again.

"At least we were there together," said Ali Baba. "You can always talk about it with me. Or I can talk about it with you."

"What did he whisper to you?" Natalie asked. "Is it a secret?"

"I can tell you," said Ali Baba. "He said, 'Happy Hanukkah.' "

5. ALI BABA ON HIS OWN

When Ali Baba Bernstein was nine years, seven months, and twenty-four days old, he had a runny nose and a tickle in his throat. It was not a serious illness, but since it was a cold, damp day outside, Mrs. Bernstein felt strongly that her son should not go to school.

"An ounce of prevention is worth a pound of cure," she reminded him.

"I'd like a pound of salami and an ounce of

mustard," said Ali Baba. He was not very sick at all. He rather thought it would be fun to stay home on this ordinary Thursday. His teacher, Ms. Melrose, had been absent for the past two days herself, and Ali Baba didn't like the teacher who had been called in to substitute.

"I don't have any salami, but you can have a frankfurter for lunch," offered his mother.

"It's too early to be talking about lunch," said Mr. Bernstein as he finished his breakfast before leaving for work. "Drink a lot of liquids," he instructed his son. "Tea with lemon and honey is good when you have a cold."

After Mr. Bernstein left for his office, Ali Baba's mother went to the phone. "I'm going to ask Grandma to come and stay with you for a couple of hours," she explained to her son. "Today is the day I'm scheduled to meet with the District Supervisor of the Board of Education. The Parent Teacher Association has been trying to set up this meeting for weeks, and I don't want to miss it."

Ali Baba nodded. His mother was on the Executive Board of the PTA, and next year she was going to be the group's president. Unfortunately it turned out that Ali Baba and Ms. Melrose were not the only people who were ill that day. Both of Ali Baba's grandparents seemed to have colds, too.

Whenever his parents went out at night, Elliot, a high-school student who lived in their building, stayed with Ali Baba. But on a Thursday morning Elliot was off at school. "There must be someone who can stay with you," said Mrs. Bernstein as she turned the pages in her address book.

"I can stay by myself. I'm not a baby anymore," protested Ali Baba between sneezes. He liked the idea of being in charge of himself like a grown-up.

Mrs. Bernstein was not convinced. But she couldn't find a substitute baby-sitter, and she didn't want to miss her meeting.

"All right," she agreed at last, reluctantly. "I won't really be gone very long—two hours at the most."

"Hey," protested Ali Baba, "I'm almost ten years old. I can be on my own without any problem. I'm not a baby."

Mrs. Bernstein showed Ali Baba where the package of frankfurters was in the refrigerator. "Just put one in a pot and cover it with water," she instructed him. "When the water boils, you'll know the frankfurter is ready."

"Sure," said Ali Baba. He was lucky that they had an electric stove. His friend Roger could never do any cooking unless his parents were around to watch, because they had a gas stove, and so there was a real flame under the cooking pots. They thought a real flame was dangerous. Ali Baba knew his parents would think so, too.

"I'll phone Mr. Salmon and tell him that you're here on your own," said Mrs. Bernstein. "You can call him if you need anything." Ali Baba had gone running in the park quite regularly with Mr. Salmon, and the two had become good friends. He was almost as proud as his neighbor at all the weight the man had lost recently. But still, he knew he wouldn't phone him today. He liked the idea of taking care of himself.

After his mother left, Ali Baba went to his

bedroom and sat down on his bed. He was going to read his library book, but as he sat there looking around, he got an idea. His bedroom was a boring place. His bed had been against the same wall for as long as he could remember. It was across from his bookcase and a chest of drawers. Ali Baba thought he would like to rearrange the furniture. Wouldn't his mother be surprised when she came home and found he had shifted all the furniture!

Ali Baba got off the bed and began to move it across the room. It wasn't too heavy, so he was able to push it. But when he got it partway across the room, he realized that the bookcase and the chest of drawers were in the way. He saw at once that he couldn't move the bookcase with all the books on it. So he began taking books off the shelves. The bottom shelf had several big, flat picture books from when he was little. He sat on the floor and looked at them. Then he removed the other books and put them on the floor, too.

When all the books were off the bookcase,

Ali Baba moved it across the room. He sneezed several times as he was carrying the case across the room, but at last he succeeded in placing it where the bed had been before. The bed was still in the middle of the room because the chest of drawers was blocking it from the new location that Ali Baba planned for it.

He had to remove all the drawers from the chest before he could attempt to move it. All these efforts were making him very hot and thirsty. He remembered that his father had told him to drink a lot of liquids. So he went into the kitchen to pour himself a drink. There was a container of orange juice, but as he reached for it, Ali Baba noticed the bottle of chocolate syrup. Chocolate milk would taste really great just now.

Ali Baba removed both the bottle of chocolate syrup and the container of milk from the refrigerator. He took a glass from the cupboard and poured about an inch of syrup into the glass. The thick, dark brown syrup looked yummy. He decided to pour just a little more syrup into the glass to make the milk extra chocolaty. It occurred to Ali Baba that a whole glass of chocolate syrup would be liquid and would be good for him. So Ali Baba kept filling the glass with syrup and then lifted it to his lips. He knew his mother would never approve, but she didn't know what was really good.

The first mouthful of chocolate syrup was wonderful. Ali Baba held the syrup in his mouth to savor the thick liquid. He swallowed and took another gulp. The second mouthful seemed less wonderful, and it was hard to swallow. Somehow Ali Baba didn't even want to take another swallow. He poured the rest of the syrup down the drain and rinsed out the glass. He filled it with water and drank. He felt a little sick. Probably he should have settled for orange juice today, especially since he had a cold.

Ali Baba went back to his bedroom. His books were all over the floor, and the drawers from the chest were on the floor, too. He pushed the bed into the new location. But when it was there, he realized something he had never been aware of before. The closet was in the middle of this wall. And now the end of Ali Baba's bed was blocking the door. It would be impossible to ever open the closet door if the bed remained in this new place. That meant that Ali Baba would have to push everything back to the way it was before.

He didn't feel like doing that just now. He went into the living room and left the mess in his bedroom behind him. He turned on the television set. He rarely had a chance to watch daytime television. Perhaps there was a super program on right now. Unfortunately, the Bernsteins' set was not working too well lately. The picture bounced up and down in black and white. Ali Baba changed the channel. Sometimes one channel worked, even when another one didn't. However, although Ali Baba switched the dial from one channel to another, none of them worked very well. Perhaps he could adjust one of the buttons in the back of the machine.

He turned one of the switches in the back and waited to see if the picture improved. It didn't, but the program was a rerun of one of Ali Baba's favorite shows. Even though he knew just what was going to happen, he sat down to watch. It was a little disconcerting to have the picture bouncing up and down, but Ali Baba wanted to hear his favorite exchange toward the end of the show, when the actor pretended to speak French and made up a lot of nonsense words. He thought he must have seen this show at least half a dozen times over the past couple of years, and every time he found the ending hilariously funny.

The wobbly picture on the screen began to hurt Ali Baba's eyes. Just as the actor was about to begin his phony French, the telephone rang. Ali Baba went to answer it. It was his mother, checking to be sure that everything was all right.

"Our TV is the one that's really sick," Ali Baba complained. He was annoyed that he had missed his favorite part of the show.

He went back to the living room. He turned off the set and went into his bedroom. The mess was not inviting. Ali Baba turned away and went toward the kitchen. His head was

aching, and his stomach didn't feel too great, either. Still, once in the kitchen, he remembered the frankfurter in the refrigerator. Maybe he would feel better if he ate his lunch.

Ali Baba filled a small pot with water and put the frankfurter inside. He took a slice of whole-wheat bread out of the refrigerator. Too bad his mother didn't have any frankfurter buns. He got the jar of mustard from the shelf in the refrigerator door, then he took a couple of cherry tomatoes, too.

When the water boiled and the frankfurter was cooked, Ali Baba turned off the stove. He stabbed the frankfurter with a fork and put it in the center of the slice of bread. He spread a thick layer of mustard on the frank and folded the bread in half. He took a big bite. It tasted pretty good. He guessed he was a better cook than he had ever realized. However, when he had finished eating the frankfurter and bread and the cherry tomatoes, he realized that his stomach still felt bad. His headache was still bothering him, too, and his throat felt scratchier than ever.

Ali Baba remembered what his father had

said about a cup of hot tea with lemon and honey. Perhaps the tea would cure him of all his ailments. He went to the stove and saw the pot half-filled with water in which he had cooked his frankfurter. So instead of filling the tea kettle with water, he turned on the stove and reheated the water he had used to cook the frankfurter. He would save time by using that same water because it was still quite warm.

While the water boiled, Ali Baba looked for the jar of honey in the cupboard and for some lemon. He got a mug and put a spoonful of honey in it. Then he got a tea bag and put that in the mug, too. When the water had reboiled, he poured some on top of the honey and the tea bag. He couldn't find any lemon, so he stirred the tea and honey and water and blew on it gently, waiting for it to cool a little. Then he took a sip.

For some reason, the tea had a greasy taste. It was a little like drinking a liquid, sweetened frankfurter. He took two sips and then poured the rest down the drain. Now he felt like throwing up. In the bathroom, Ali Baba waited. But he didn't throw up after all. He just stood there thinking about it. His stomach felt bad. His head felt bad and his throat felt bad. He sneezed a couple of times and his eyes watered from the effort. He decided to lie down on his bed and rest.

He had to climb over all the books and the drawers that were still on the floor. Later, when he was feeling better, he would have to put everything back the way it was before. He lay on his bed and wished his mother would come home. It was hard work taking care of himself.

It was only another half-hour till Mrs. Bernstein returned home. She was pleased with the way her meeting had gone. On the way home she had stopped for some groceries. "I have lemons to make you some tea with honey," she said. "It will make you feel better."

Ali Baba sat up in bed. "I feel awful," he said.

Mrs. Bernstein came into the bedroom. "This room looks awful," she exclaimed. "What went on here while I was gone?"

"I thought I'd move the furniture around, but it doesn't fit," explained Ali Baba.

"Did you have your lunch?" she asked.

Ali Baba nodded. "It was okay," he said. "But you cook better than I do."

"That's all right. You're only nine," said Mrs. Bernstein, removing her hand from his forehead. "You don't have any fever," she said, smiling at him. "And you'll learn how to take care of yourself better as you get older."

Later, because Ali Baba wasn't feeling too well, his parents put all the furniture back in its proper location in the bedroom. They even put the books back on the shelves and the drawers back in the chest. When they were finished, everything looked just as it had in the morning. Ali Baba decided that he liked his room as it was—especially since nothing was on the floor waiting for him to pick it up.

For supper his mother made a pot of chicken soup. Ali Baba didn't know if chicken soup really could cure a cold, but it certainly tasted a whole lot better than the glass of chocolate syrup and the greasy tea he had drunk earlier in the day. There was time enough for him to be on his own when he was ten, he decided.

6. ALI BABA AND THE MYSTERY OF THE MISSING CIRCUS TICKETS

On the Sunday morning when Ali Baba was nine years, eleven months, and four days old, his best friend, Roger Zucker, was ten years old. As a birthday treat, Roger's parents had bought three tickets to the circus. Originally the plan was for both parents to take Roger. But then Roger's little sister, Sarah, who was nicknamed Sugar, got the chicken pox. So Mrs. Zucker said that she would stay home with Sugar instead of leaving her with a baby-sitter. And that meant there was an extra ticket. Roger phoned at nine-thirty in the morning and invited Ali Baba to go with him and his father.

"Super!" shouted Ali Baba into the telephone. What great luck that Sugar had gotten the chicken pox!

Ali Baba and Roger had both had chicken pox already. They had caught it two years ago when almost the entire second grade had had the disease. But Sugar, who wasn't born at the time, had not caught it then. Ali Baba did a happy little dance around the kitchen. He loved the circus and couldn't wait till the afternoon.

Then the phone rang again. It was Roger.

"You didn't change your mind, did you?" asked Ali Baba nervously. Perhaps Roger was going to invite someone else instead. Or maybe Sugar had miraculously recovered.

"No, but something terrible has happened," said Roger. "My mother can't find the tickets. She said they were in her pocketbook, but they aren't there now."

"Maybe she put them someplace else," suggested Ali Baba.

"No. She says she's certain that she put

them right in her pocketbook when she bought them a couple of days ago. And she called the ticket office and they told her they've sold out all the tickets. This is the last performance, so we can't go to the circus after all." Roger sounded miserable. "This is turning out to be a rotten birthday," he said.

"Wait," said Ali Baba. "I'm coming over. We'll search your house. If they weren't stolen, we'll find them."

He hung up the phone and raced to get his jacket. "I'm going over to Roger's house," he informed his mother. And then, without any further explanation, he rushed out.

Ali Baba wanted to go to the circus very much. But there was something that he loved even more than the circus. He loved mysteries. And here were both at the same time. A mystery about the tickets, which if he solved it would mean that he would get his afternoon entertainment, too. But he had to work fast. It was already after ten o'clock. The circus was scheduled to begin at two. He had less than four hours to locate the missing tickets.

"Are you sure you put the tickets in your

pocketbook?" he grilled Mrs. Zucker when he got to Roger's house. Mrs. Zucker was sitting at the kitchen table with the entire contents of her pocketbook spilled onto the table. There were her keys, sunglasses, wallet, a small notebook, a makeup case, and a package of sugarless gum. There were no circus tickets.

"I know!" said Ali Baba suddenly. "You were carrying a different pocketbook when you bought the tickets!"

It was a good idea on his part. His mother had several different pocketbooks, and which one she carried depended on which outfit she was wearing. (And Ali Baba noticed that her keys were almost always in a pocketbook that she wasn't carrying.)

Mrs. Zucker shook her head. "The handle just came off my other bag," she said. "I have to get it repaired or replaced. This is the only pocketbook I've used for thc past two weeks."

Roger sighed.

"Where do you leave your pocketbook when you are at home?" asked Ali Baba. "Did anyone touch it? Could Sugar have taken the tickets out? I don't mean she stole them, but she could have taken them to play with, couldn't she?" he asked.

"I keep my pocketbook on a shelf in the closet. She can't reach it," explained Mrs. Zucker. "Besides, even if she could, she wouldn't be able to open the clasp on the bag."

Ali Baba sighed.

"I'm looking to see if there is a good movie playing," called Mr. Zucker from the next room. He had the newspaper open before him and had promised the boys to take them to a film as a consolation. But neither boy wanted a movie. What was a movie compared to the circus?

"Could you have put the tickets in your pocket?" Ali Baba suggested. "Did you look in your coat pocket?"

Mrs. Zucker gasped. "I think you're right!" she said, jumping up. "I think I stuffed the tickets into my raincoat pocket. How silly of me to forget." She jumped up and went to the closet. "See, here they are," she said, pulling an envelope out of the pocket. However, the envelope did not contain circus tickets. There were grocery coupons to get fifteen and twenty cents off on cat food and coffee and things like that.

"How did these get into my pocket?" Mrs. Zucker asked. She inspected the coat closely. "This isn't my coat," she exclaimed.

"Whose coat is it?" asked Ali Baba excitedly. This mystery was getting more and more mysterious.

Mrs. Zucker shrugged her shoulders. "I don't know," she said. "I guess someone took my coat from the closet and left this one instead."

"How can we find out who it was?" asked Roger.

Just then the telephone rang. Mrs. Zucker went to answer it as Roger and Ali Baba stood looking at each other helplessly.

"It's here! I have it!" Mrs. Zucker shouted happily into the phone. "I'll have Roger bring it over to you right away."

She hung up the receiver and smiled brightly. "Your worries are over," she said. "That was Rosie Relkin. She was here last night with some of our other friends for coffee

and dessert. And she accidentally took the wrong raincoat when she went home. So all you have to do is drop off this one at her apartment and get mine."

"Did you ask her if there were circus tickets in the pocket?" asked Roger.

"Don't be silly," said his mother. "Of course the tickets are in the pocket. You'll see for yourself as soon as you get the coat."

"Let's get going," said Ali Baba. "Where does Rosie Relkin live?"

It was only two blocks to Rosie Relkin's apartment. She opened the door as soon as the boys rang the bell. She had been waiting for them.

"Here," said Roger, exchanging the tan raincoat in his arms for the one Rosie Relkin held out. Roger put his hands into the pockets and immediately pulled out an envelope addressed to Kit Conners and a subway token. But there were no circus tickets.

"Where are the tickets? They're not in either pocket," said Roger, mystified. "And what is this letter doing in my mother's pocket?"

"That can't be your mother's coat," Ali Baba said. "It must belong to someone named Kit Conners."

"This isn't my coat, either," said Rosie Relkin, handing back the coat that Roger had given her. "Mine has a red plaid lining. This is blue."

Roger took one raincoat, and Ali Baba took the other. "Who do they belong to?" Ali Baba asked.

"And what about the circus tickets?" asked Roger.

"I bet Kit Conners took my coat," said Rosie Relkin. "She was at the Zuckers' apartment last night, too."

"What about Mrs. Zucker's coat?" asked Ali Baba. "Where do you think that is?"

Rosie Relkin shook her head. "I don't know," she said. "This is quite a tangle. But I'd really appreciate it if you took this over to Kit Conners's apartment and brought my coat to me. Kit only lives a block away."

"I wonder if we'll ever get to the circus?" Roger sighed as the two boys and the two raincoats went off in the direction of Kit Conners's apartment.

"Maybe Kit Conners has your mother's coat," said Ali Baba. "We've got to find those tickets before two o'clock."

"And we still have to find Rosie Relkin's raincoat for her, too," Roger said.

"You know something?" said Ali Baba. "If I were president of the United States, I would make a law against these tan raincoats. Why does everyone wear the same kind of coat?"

Kit Conners was delighted to see the boys. "Rosie Relkin phoned to tell me you were coming. She said you had my coat. I didn't realize that I had taken the wrong one last night. But I looked now, and sure enough, I've got someone else's."

She took the coat that Roger gave her. "It's mine, all right," she said. "I wonder whose coat I wore home last night?"

"It must be my mother's," said Roger.

"It might belong to Rosie Relkin," Ali Baba reminded his friend. "Her coat is still missing, too."

Kit Conners handed Roger a coat that was a clone of the one that he had given her. However, on closer inspection, the lining was different. "It's not Rosie Relkin's raincoat," said Ali Baba. The lining was green plaid.

"I never noticed what color lining my mother's coat had," said Roger. "Up until today it never mattered. But I sure hope the lining of her coat is green plaid and that this is it." He put his hands inside the pockets of the coat that Kit Conners had handed him. "What's this?" he asked.

"Let's see," demanded Ali Baba.

Roger handed Ali Baba a baby's pacifier.

"Does your sister still use one of these?" asked Ali Baba.

"No," said Roger with disgust. "She outgrew it ages ago."

"Margie and George Upchurch were at your house last night," Kit Conners told Roger. "They have a six-month-old baby. I bet this coat belongs to Margie. Let me give you her address."

"Your parents have too many friends," complained Ali Baba.

A minute later the boys were off looking for the street where the Upchurch family lived.

"That can't be my coat," said Margie Upchurch when Ali Baba and Roger Zucker tried explaining about the mix-up of the raincoats the night before. "I wore my coat home," she shouted above the wails of a crying baby.

In the background Ali Baba could see Mr. Upchurch, unshaven and still in his bathrobe, trying to comfort the infant.

"It must be your coat," said Ali Baba. "There was a pacifier in the pocket, and we can see you have a baby."

Mrs. Upchurch looked surprised at this piece of information. "A pacifier?" she asked with delight. "We've been looking all over the house for one of the baby's pacifiers, and they've all disappeared." She examined the object that Roger handed her.

"Let me just go and wash it," she shouted above the baby's cries. A minute later the clean pacifier was in the baby's mouth and all was quiet. Then Margie Upchurch went to her closet and took out still another tan raincoat.

"I don't know who this one belongs to," she said.

Roger looked at the coat hopefully. "You look," he told Ali Baba. "I'm scared."

Ali Baba wasn't scared at all. He was confident that they had finally tracked down the correct coat. He put his hands into the pockets and triumphantly pulled out a small envelope from one of them. Inside there were three tan tickets for that afternoon's circus performance. The tickets were the same color as all of the coats.

"Hurray! We did it! We found the tickets!" he began shouting. Of all the mysteries he had ever attempted to solve, this had been the most successful.

But there was still one small mystery before the boys.

"Whose raincoat is this?" asked Margie Upchurch, pointing to the other one that was still unclaimed.

"We don't know. It isn't Rosie Relkin's," said Roger. He pulled the envelope with the grocery coupons out of the mystery raincoat. "These could belong to anyone."

"Not just anyone," Ali Baba pointed out. "They must belong to someone who has a cat."

"Muriel and Alfred Thomas were at your house last night," Margie Upchurch told

Roger. "And they have a cat," she added. "I can't ever go to their house because I have an allergy to cats. They make my eyes tear and make me sneeze, too." She went off to check the exact address where the Thomases lived.

Muriel Thomas was just as surprised as Mrs. Upchurch to discover that she had taken the wrong raincoat the evening before. She traded coats with Roger, giving him a coat with a red lining in exchange for the one he carried with a blue lining. And then the boys retraced their steps and returned to Rosie Relkin's apartment.

"Thank goodness you found it!" Rosie Relkin said, clutching her raincoat as if it were a very precious item.

Ali Baba thought that was very funny. It wasn't as if she had lost something unique. All the coats looked the same—what difference did it make what color the lining was? Once you put the coat on, no one could see the lining inside.

To the boys the unique coat was the one with the circus tickets in the pocket. Ali Baba and Roger Zucker ran all the way back to the Zucker apartment.

"I'm glad you got my coat from Rosie Relkin," said Mrs. Zucker when she saw the boys.

"We didn't get it from Rosie Relkin," announced Roger.

"What do you mean?" asked Mrs. Zucker.

"It will take too long to explain," said Roger. "We've got to hurry if we're going to get to the circus on time."

But there was still enough time for Ali Baba to phone home and tell his parents that he was going off to the circus with Roger. They also had time enough to admire Sugar's chicken pox and to eat a quick lunch. And finally Mr. Zucker, Roger, and Ali Baba were off to the circus.

"How does it feel being ten?" Mr. Zucker asked his son as the three of them rode downtown on the bus.

"I don't know," Roger complained. "I've been too busy this morning to think about it."

"We sure solved a big mystery," said Ali Baba proudly. He felt like a real private eye. Imagine, a mystery and a circus all on the same day. It was super!